A Note to Parents and Caregivers:

Read-it! Joke Books are for children who are moving ahead on the amazing road to reading. These fun books support the acquisition and extension of reading skills as well as a love of books.

Published by the same company that produces *Read-it!* Readers, these books introduce the question/answer pattern that helps children expand their thinking about language structure and book formats.

When sharing a book with your child, read in short stretches, pausing often to talk about the pictures and the meaning of the book. The question/answer format works well for this purpose and provides an opportunity to talk about the language and meaning of the jokes. Have your child turn the pages and point to the pictures and familiar words. Read the story in a natural voice; have fun creating the voices of characters or emphasizing some important words. And be sure to reread favorite parts.

There is no right or wrong way to share books with children. Find time to read with your child, and pass on the legacy of literacy.

Adria F. Klein, Ph.D.
Professor Emeritus
California State University
San Bernardino, California

Managing Editor: Bob Temple
Creative Director: Terri Foley
Editors: Brenda Haugen, Nadia Higgins
Designer: John Moldstad
Page production: Picture Window Books
The illustrations in this book were prepared digitally.

Picture Window Books
5115 Excelsior Boulevard
Suite 232
Minneapolis, MN 55416
1-877-845-8392
www.picturewindowbooks.com

Printed in the United States of America.

Library of Congress Cataloging-in-Publication Data
Dahl, Michael.
Door knockers : a book of knock-knock jokes / written by Michael Dahl ;
illustrated by Brian Jensen ; reading advisers, Adria F. Klein, Susan Kesselring.
p. cm. — (Read-it! joke books)
ISBN 1-4048-0238-X
1. Knock-knock jokes. I. Jensen, Brian, 1959- II. Title.
PN6231.K55 D344 2003
818'.602—dc21

2003004868

Door Knockers

A Book of Knock-Knock Jokes

Michael Dahl • Illustrated by Brian Jensen

Reading Advisers:
Adria F. Klein, Ph.D.
Professor Emeritus, California State University
San Bernardino, California

Susan Kesselring, M.A., Literacy Educator
Rosemount-Apple Valley-Eagan (Minnesota) School District

PICTURE WINDOW BOOKS
Minneapolis, Minnesota

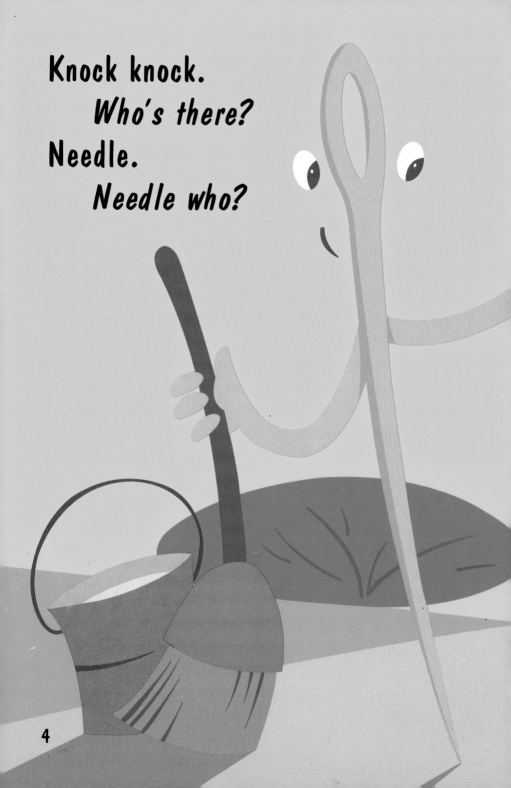

Knock knock.
    Who's there?
Needle.
    Needle who?

4

Needle little help
around the house?

Knock knock.
 Who's there?
Major.
 Major who?

6 Major open the door, didn't I?

Knock knock.
Who's there?
Sherwood.
Sherwood who?

Sherwood like to come inside.　7

Knock knock.
    Who's there?
Catsup.
    Catsup who?

Catsup

Catsup in the tree!

Knock knock.
    Who's there?
Arthur.
    Arthur who?

Arthur any cookies left?

9

Knock knock.
    Who's there?
Zombies.
    Zombies who?

Honey

Zombies make honey,
and zombies just buzz.   11

Knock knock.
    Who's there?
Ben.
    Ben who?

12   Ben looking all over for you.

Knock knock.
  Who's there?
Marsha.
  Marsha who?

Marsha Mallow.

Knock knock.
  Who's there?
Orange juice.
  Orange juice who?

Orange juice going
    to let me in?

Knock knock.
Who's there?
Beehive.
Beehive who?

Beehive yourself,
or you'll get hurt!

Knock knock.
    Who's there?
Omar.
    Omar who?

Omar goodness,
wrong door! Sorry!

Knock knock.
    Who's there?
Gus.
    Gus who?

Gus who's coming to dinner?

Knock knock.
    Who's there?
Sultan.
    Sultan who?

Sultan Pepper.   19

Knock knock.
Who's there?
Stopwatch.
Stopwatch who?

Stopwatch you're doing,
and let me in!

Knock knock.
    Who's there?
Duck.
    Duck who?

Duck! The neighbors
are throwing snowballs!

21

Knock knock.
 Who's there?
A herd.
 A herd who?

A herd you were home,
so I came over.

Knock knock.
　　Who's there?
Alma.
　　Alma who?

24　　　Alma candy's gone!